T0011010

Published in 2022 by OH!
An Imprint of Welbeck Non-Fiction Limited,
part of Welbeck Publishing Group.
Based in London and Sydney.
www.welbeckpublishing.com

ISBN 978-1-80069-196-4

Compiled and written by: Stella Caldwell
Design: Zoe Mercer
Project manager: Russell Porter
Production: Jess Brisley

A CIP catalogue record for this book is available from the British Library

Printed in China

10 9 8 7 6 5 4 3 2 1

Cover illustration by Cristiano Siqueira
Raven drawings by Alfmaler / Shutterstock

THE LITTLE BOOK OF

EDGAR ALLAN POE

THE LITTLE BOOK OF
EDGAR ALLAN POE

DARK ROMANCE FROM THE
MASTER OF THE MACABRE

CONTENTS

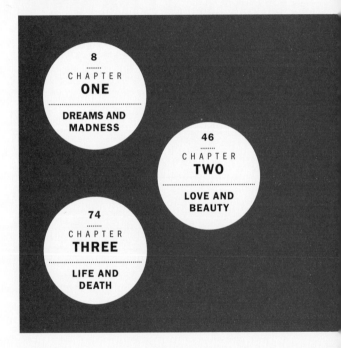

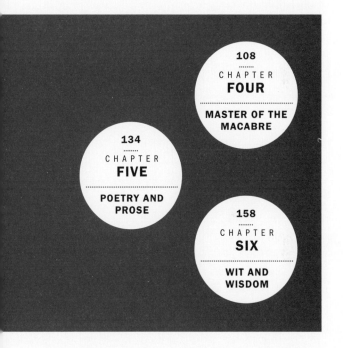

INTRODUCTION

In 1849, at the age of 40, the American author Edgar
Allan Poe was found slumped in the streets of Baltimore.
Barely conscious and dressed in somebody else's
clothes, he was admitted to hospital. Gripped by fevered
hallucinations, he died a few days later.

Poe's mysterious death has only cemented his
reputation as the father of gothic horror. But while he is
chiefly remembered for the dark imaginings that haunted
his unsettling poems and tales, he is also celebrated as
the architect of the modern short story, as the inventor
of detective fiction, and as an accomplished editor and
literary critic.

Poe's life was turbulent. Before he was three, his father
had abandoned the family and his mother had died of
tuberculosis. Brought up by a wealthy couple, Poe didn't get
on with his foster father and was eventually cut from his will.
At the age of 27, he married his 13-year-old cousin. Her death,

at the age of 24, sent Poe spiralling into deep despair.

Poe's first literary efforts were as a poet. To improve his earnings, he turned to fiction, winning a short story competition in 1933. He soon found himself working for a literary journal, where he developed a reputation as a savage critic, and began publishing some of his best-known works, including "The Fall of the House of Usher," "The Murders in the Rue Morgue," and "The Raven." Although poverty would remain a constant feature throughout Poe's life, he was the first major American writer to earn a living through writing alone. Today, his influence on world literature is undisputed.

Showcasing quotes from Poe's short stories, poems, essays, and letters, and complemented by fascinating facts about his life, this little book teems with mystery, madness and the macabre. It is a fine celebration of one of the most singular talents in American literature.

CHAPTER
ONE

DREAMS AND
MADNESS

"**T**hose who dream by day are cognizant of many things which escape those who dream only by night. In their gray visions they obtain glimpses of eternity, and thrill, in waking, to find that they have been upon the verge of the great secret. In snatches, they learn something of the wisdom which is of good, and more of the mere knowledge which is of evil.

"ELEONORA," 1841

Edgar Poe (he did not acquire his middle name, Allan, until later in his life) was born in Boston, US, in 1809.

His parents were both actors who had played roles in Shakespeare's *King Lear*. Some have speculated that they named their son for the play's character Edgar, the son of the Earl of Gloucester.

Poe's father abandoned his family in 1810, and his mother died from tuberculosis the following year. The young Poe was separated from his siblings, William and Rosalie, and sent to live with a tobacco merchant and his wife, John and Frances Allan.

They never formally adopted him but had him baptized as Edgar "Allan" Poe in 1812.

"We gave the Future to the winds, and slumbered tranquilly in the Present, weaving the dull world around us into dreams."

**"THE MYSTERY OF MARIE ROGÊT,"
1842**

"It is a happiness to wonder; —it is a happiness to dream."

"MORELLA," 1835

"It is by no means an irrational fancy that, in a future existence, we shall look upon what we think our present existence, as a dream."

"MARGINALIA," 1836

Illustration for "The Pit and the Pendulum," by Harry Clarke, 1919

"Arousing from the most profound of slumbers, we break the gossamer web of some dream. Yet in a second afterward, (so frail may that web have been) we remember not that we have dreamed."

**"THE PIT AND THE PENDULUM,"
1842**

"**A**nd the Raven, never flitting, still is sitting,
    still is sitting
On the pallid bust of Pallas just above my
    chamber door;
And his eyes have all the seeming of a
    demon's that is dreaming,
And the lamp-light o'er him streaming throws
    his shadow on the floor..."

"THE RAVEN," 1845

"A dark unfathomed tide
Of interminable pride—
A mystery, and a dream,
Should my early life seem;
I say that dream was fraught
With a wild and waking thought
Of beings that have been,
Which my spirit hath not seen,
Had I let them pass me by,
With a dreaming eye!"

"IMITATION," 1827

Illustration for "The Black Cat," by H. Meyer, 1884

"**F**or the most wild, yet most homely narrative which I am about to pen, I neither expect nor solicit belief. Mad indeed would I be to expect it, in a case where my very senses reject their own evidence. Yet, mad am I not—and very surely do I not dream. But to-morrow I die, and to-day I would unburthen my soul."

"THE BLACK CAT," 1843

"If you determine to abandon me—here take I [my] farewell—Neglected—I will be doubly ambitious, & the world shall hear of the son whom you have thought unworthy of your notice."

LETTER TO HIS FOSTER FATHER, JOHN ALLAN, DECEMBER 22, 1828

Poe had a difficult relationship with his foster father, John Allan, who described him as "lazy ... sulky, & ill-tempered." Allan disapproved of Poe's literary ambitions and refused to finance his studies at university. In an effort to make money, Poe turned to gambling but instead amassed debts. Allan's refusal to help him through this period was the start of a bitter feud that ended with Allan cutting Poe out of his will.

It would be easy to assume that the teenage Poe was a stay-at-home, angst-ridden loner, but he was in fact an accomplished athlete. He enjoyed running, boxing, and rowing, and he was renowned among his friends for swimming six miles upriver in Virginia's Charles River.

"From childhood's hour I have not been
As others were—I have not seen
As others saw—I could not bring
My passions from a common spring—
From the same source I have not taken
My sorrow—I could not awaken
My heart to joy at the same tone—
And all I lov'd—I lov'd alone—"

**FROM "ALONE," WRITTEN WHEN POE WAS 21,
AND PUBLISHED IN 1875**

"**A**nd all my days are trances,
And all my nightly dreams
Are where thy grey eye glances,
And where thy footstep gleams—
In what ethereal dances,
By what eternal streams."

"TO ONE IN PARADISE," 1834

"I became insane, with long intervals of horrible sanity."

LETTER TO GEORGE WASHINGTON EVELETH, 1846

"**I** was never really insane except upon occasions when my heart was touched."

LETTER TO HIS AUNT MARIA CLEMM, JULY 7, 1849

"**M**en have called me mad; but the question is not yet settled, whether madness is or is not the loftiest intelligence..."

"ELEONORA," 1842

"In visions of the dark night
I have dreamed of joy departed—
But a waking dream of life and light
Hath left me broken-hearted."

"A DREAM," 1829

"**D**reams! in their vivid coloring of life
As in that fleeting, shadowy, misty strife
Of semblance with reality which brings
To the delirious eye, more lovely things
Of Paradise and Love—and all our own!
Than young Hope in his sunniest hour
hath known."

"DREAMS," 1828

In 1827, Poe published a collection of Byronic poetry called *Tamerlane and Other Poems*—the work was attributed to "A Bostonian."

Only 50 copies were printed, and the poems received no critical attention. The volume is now recognized as one of the rarest first editions in American literature.

"**Y**ou call it hope—that fire of fire!
It is but agony of desire..."

"TAMERLANE," 1827

"**W**hen a madman appears thoroughly sane, indeed, it is high time to put him in a straight jacket."

"THE SYSTEM OF DOCTOR TARR AND PROFESSOR FETHER," 1845

"True!—nervous—very, very dreadfully nervous I had been and am; but why will you say that I am mad?"

"THE TELL-TALE HEART," 1843

Illustration for "The Tell-Tale Heart," by Arthur Rackham, 1935

" **I** have absolutely no pleasure in the stimulants in which I sometimes so madly indulge. It has not been in the pursuit of pleasure that I have periled life and reputation and reason. It has been in the desperate attempt to escape from torturing memories—memories of wrong and injustice and imputed dishonor—from a sense of insupportable loneliness and a dread of some strange impending doom."

**LETTER TO POET SARAH H. WHITMAN,
NOVEMBER 3, 1848**

Poe was a pioneer of the short story, but he was also a superb poet, exploring themes of love, death, and regret. Here are ten of his best:

The Raven
Annabel Lee
To Helen
Lenore
A Dream Within a Dream
The Bells
Eldorado
The Haunted Palace
The City in the Sea
Alone

"That which you mistake for madness is but an over acuteness of the senses."

"THE TELL-TALE HEART," 1843

"I call to mind flatness and dampness; and then all is madness—the madness of a memory which busies itself among forbidden things."

"THE PIT AND THE PENDULUM," 1842

After dropping out of university, Poe enlisted in the army under the name of Edgar A. Perry. He made a good soldier, becoming an officer cadet at the West Point military academy two years later.

Poe soon tired of the studying and rigid discipline, though, and after deliberately breaking the rules and missing his classes, was expelled.

"**N**ow this is the point. You fancy me mad. Madmen know nothing. But you should have seen me. You should have seen how wisely I proceeded..."

"THE TELL-TALE HEART," 1843

"**H**ad the routine of our life at this place been known to the world, we should have been regarded as madmen—although, perhaps, as madmen of a harmless nature."

**"THE MURDERS IN THE RUE MORGUE,"
1841**

Illustration for "The Murders in the Rue Morgue," by Daniel Vierge, 1870

CHAPTER
TWO

LOVE AND
BEAUTY

"**O**n desperate seas long wont to roam,
Thy hyacinth hair, thy classic face,
Thy Naiad airs have brought me home
To the glory that was Greece,
And the grandeur that was Rome."

"TO HELEN," 1831

"Thou wast that all to me, love,
For which my soul did pine—
A green isle in the sea, love,
A fountain and a shrine,
All wreathed with fairy fruits and flowers,
And all the flowers were mine."

"TO ONE IN PARADISE," 1834

EDGAR ALLAN POE

"The most natural, and, consequently, the truest and most intense of the human affections are those which arise in the heart as if by electric sympathy."

"THE SPECTACLES," 1844

"**B**eauty of whatever kind, in its supreme development, invariably excites the sensitive soul to tears."

**"THE PHILOSOPHY OF COMPOSITION",
1846**

"There is no exquisite beauty ... without some strangeness in the proportion."

"LIGEIA," 1838

Illustration for "Ligeia," by Arthur Rackham, 1935

"**O**, human love! thou spirit given,
On Earth, of all we hope in Heaven!"

"TAMERLANE," 1827

"In beauty of face no maiden ever equaled her. It was the radiance of an opium-dream— an airy and spirit-lifting vision more wildly divine than the phantasies which hovered about the slumbering souls of the daughters of Delos."

"LIGEIA", 1838

After his dismissal from the West Point military academy, Poe moved into the home of his aunt Maria Clemm and her daughter, Virginia, and began writing in earnest.

His first short story, *Metzengerstein*, was published in 1832. A supernatural tale set in a gloomy, medieval castle, it focused on a feud between two ancient families.

"The very instant you get this, come to me. The joy of seeing you will almost compensate for our sorrows. We can but die together... For your sake it would be sweet to live, but we must die together. You have been all in all to me, darling, ever beloved mother, and dearest, truest friend."

IN A LETTER TO HIS AUNT AND MOTHER-IN-LAW, MARIA CLEMM, JULY 7, 1849

"**A**lthough I saw that the features of Ligeia were not of a classic regularity—although I perceived that her loveliness was indeed 'exquisite,' and felt that there was much of 'strangeness' pervading it, yet I have tried in vain to detect the irregularity and to trace home my own perception of 'the strange.'"

"LIGEIA", 1838

Poe's older brother, Henry, was also a published poet. Although the two brothers were separated after the death of their mother, they became close again as adults. Henry, who was a heavy drinker, died at the age of 24. Poe wrote, "There can be no tie more strong than that of brother for brother—it is not so much that they love one another as that they both love the same parent."

"Thou wast all that to me, love,
For which my soul did pine—
A green isle in the sea, love,
A fountain and a shrine,
All wreathed with fairy fruits and flowers,
And all the flowers were mine."

"TO ONE IN PARADISE," 1849

"**T**here is something in the unselfish and self-sacrificing love of a brute, which goes directly to the heart of him who has had frequent occasion to test the paltry friendship and gossamer fidelity of mere Man."

"THE BLACK CAT," 1843

"**Y**ou will always have the reflection that my agony is more than I can bear—that you have driven me to the grave—for love like mine can never be gotten over ... What have I to live for? Among strangers with not one soul to love me."

**LETTER TO HIS AUNT MARIA CLEMM,
AUGUST 29, 1835**

It followed her attempt to prevent him from marrying his
13-year-old cousin, Virginia.

"**H**elen, thy beauty is to me
Like those Nicean barks of yore,
That gently, o'er a perfumed sea,
The weary, wayworn wanderer bore
To his own native shore."

"TO HELEN," 1831

Poe is often considered America's first "professional writer," eking out his living through writing alone. But despite his literary success, he struggled financially throughout his life.

He once offered a story to a magazine for publication, finishing his letter with the words, "P.S. I am poor."

"**I** have made no money. I am as poor
now as ever I was in my life—except in
hope, which is by no means bankable."

LETTER TO FREDERICK W. THOMAS, 1845

"From that hour I loved you. Yes, I now feel that it was then—on that evening of sweet dreams—that the very first dawn of human love burst upon the icy Night of my spirit. Since that period, I have never seen nor heard your name without a shiver half of delight, half of anxiety."

LETTER TO POET SARAH H. WHITMAN, WITH WHOM POE HAD A BRIEF RELATIONSHIP, 1848

"All thoughts—all passions seem now merged in that one consuming desire—the mere wish to make you comprehend—to make you see that for which there is no human voice—the unutterable fervor of my love for you."

LETTER TO SARAH H. WHITMAN, 1848

"Because I feel that, in the Heavens above,

The angels, whispering to one another,

Can find, among their burning terms of love,

None so devotional as that of 'Mother'..."

"TO MY MOTHER," 1849

"**F**or passionate love is still divine:
I lov'd her as an angel might
With ray of the all living light
Which blazes upon Edis' shrine."

"TAMERLANE," 1827

In 1835, Poe became the editor of *The Southern Literary Messenger*. It was the first of several journals that he would direct over the coming years.

The position gave him a platform from which to applaud writers he admired, and to tear down those he didn't. His brutally cutting reviews earned him the nickname "Tomahawk Man."

"**H**is [Channing's] book contains about sixty-three things, which he calls poems ... They are full of all kinds of mistakes, of which the most important is that of their having been printed at all."

"OUR AMATEUR POETS," 1849

On poet William Ellery Channing.

"**L**igeia grew ill. The wild eyes blazed with a too—too glorious effulgence; the pale fingers became of the transparent waxen hue of the grave, and the blue veins upon the lofty forehead swelled and sank impetuously with the tides of the gentle emotion. I saw that she must die..."

"LIGEIA", 1838

"Keep up your heart in all hopelessness, and trust yet a little longer."

LETTER TO HIS WIFE, VIRGINIA, JUNE 12, 1846

Written to her while she was suffering
from tuberculosis.

CHAPTER THREE

LIFE AND
DEATH

"**N**ever to suffer would never to have been blessed."

"MESMERIC REVELATION," 1849

"The boundaries which divide Life from Death are at best shadowy and vague. Who shall say where the one ends, and where the other begins?"

"THE PREMATURE BURIAL," 1844

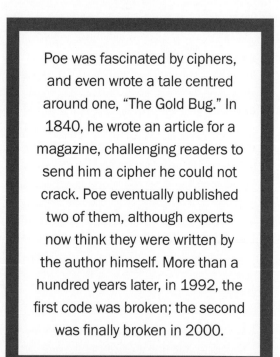

Poe was fascinated by ciphers, and even wrote a tale centred around one, "The Gold Bug." In 1840, he wrote an article for a magazine, challenging readers to send him a cipher he could not crack. Poe eventually published two of them, although experts now think they were written by the author himself. More than a hundred years later, in 1992, the first code was broken; the second was finally broken in 2000.

"Few persons can be made to believe that it is not quite an easy thing to invent a method of secret writing which shall baffle investigation. Yet it may be roundly asserted that human ingenuity cannot concoct a cipher which human ingenuity cannot resolve."

"A FEW WORDS ON SECRET WRITING," 1841

"I dread the events of the future, not in themselves but in their results."

**"THE FALL OF THE HOUSE OF USHER,"
1839**

"And so, being young and dipt in folly
I fell in love with melancholy..."

"ROMANCE," 1829

"The days have never been when thou couldst love me—but her whom in life thou didst abhor, in death thou shalt adore"

"MORELLA," 1835

"I do believe God gave me a spark of genius, but he quenched it in misery."

LETTER TO THOMAS MORRISON ALFRIEND, 1849

It was written a few weeks before Poe's death.

In 1936, when Poe was 27, he married his 13-year-old cousin, Virginia Clemm. Like much of the writer's life, the circumstances of their marriage are shrouded in mystery.

The pair seem to have been devoted to each other, though many biographers claim that the bond between them was more like brother and sister than husband and wife.

"I love, you know I love Virginia passionately, devotedly. I cannot express in words the fervent devotion I feel towards my dear little cousin—my own darling."

**LETTER TO HIS AUNT MARIA CLEMM,
AUGUST 29, 1835**

"Thank Heaven! the crisis—
The danger is past,
And the lingering illness
Is over at last—
And the fever called 'Living'
Is conquered at last."

"FOR ANNIE," 1849

"**I** could not love except where Death
Was mingling his with Beauty's breath
Or Hymen, Time, and Destiny
Were stalking between her and me."

"ROMANCE," 1829

"**I** have no faith in human perfectibility. I think that human exertion will have no appreciable effect upon humanity. Man is now only more active—not more happy—nor more wise, than he was 6,000 years ago."

**LETTER TO JAMES RUSSELL LOWELL,
JULY 2, 1844**

"**T**here are two bodies—the rudimental and the complete; corresponding with the two conditions of the worm and the butterfly. What we call 'death' is but the painful metamorphosis. Our present incarnation is progressive, preparatory, temporary. Our future is perfected, ultimate, immortal. The ultimate life is the full design.

"MESMERIC REVELATION," 1849

Illustration for "The Masque of the Red Death," by Arthue Rackham, 1935

"**A**nd Darkness and Decay and the Red Death held illimitable dominion over all."

"THE MASQUE OF THE RED DEATH,"
1842

EDGAR ALLAN POE

"**M**an's real life is happy, chiefly because he is ever expecting that it soon will be so."

MARGINALIA, 1844

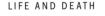

LIFE AND DEATH

"In the deepest slumber-no! In delirium-no!
In a swoon-no! In death-no! Even in the grave
all is not lost."

"THE PIT AND THE PENDULUM," 1842

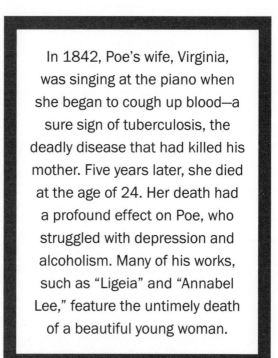

In 1842, Poe's wife, Virginia, was singing at the piano when she began to cough up blood—a sure sign of tuberculosis, the deadly disease that had killed his mother. Five years later, she died at the age of 24. Her death had a profound effect on Poe, who struggled with depression and alcoholism. Many of his works, such as "Ligeia" and "Annabel Lee," feature the untimely death of a beautiful young woman.

"But we loved with a love that was
more than love—
I and my Annabel Lee—
With a love that the wingèd seraphs of
Heaven
Coveted her and me."

"ANNABEL LEE," 1842

"Deep in earth my love is lying
And I must weep alone."

MARGINALIA, 1847

Faintly penciled on a manuscript of "Eulalie," a poem
about a happy marriage. It was probably written soon after
the funeral of Poe's wife on February 2, 1847.

"There are some secrets which do not permit themselves to be told. Men die nightly in their beds, wringing the hands of ghostly confessors, and looking them piteously in the eyes—die with despair of heart and convulsion of throat, on account of the hideousness of mysteries which will not suffer themselves to be revealed."

"THE MAN OF THE CROWD," 1840

"The happiest day—the happiest hour
My seared and blighted heart hath known,
The highest hope of pride and power,
I feel hath flown."

"THE HAPPIEST DAY," 1827

"I stand amid the roar
Of a surf-tormented shore,
And I hold within my hand
Grains of the golden sand—
How few! yet how they creep
Through my fingers to the deep,
While I weep—while I weep!"

"A DREAM WITHIN A DREAM," 1849

"Come! let the burial rite be read—the
funeral song be sung!—
An anthem for the queenliest dead that ever
died so young—
A dirge for her the doubly dead in that she
died so young."

"LENORE," 1831

Illustration for "Lenore," by Henry Sandham, 1885

"Yes, Heaven is thine; but this
Is a world of sweets and sours;
Our flowers are merely—flowers.
And the shadow of thy perfect bliss
Is the sunshine of ours."

"ISRAFEL," 1831

"**E**ven with the utterly lost, to whom life and death are equally jests, there are matters of which no jest can be made."

"THE MASQUE OF THE RED DEATH," 1842

"In the death of what was my life, then, I receive a new but—oh God! how melancholy an existence."

LETTER TO GEORGE W. EVELETH, JANUARY 4, 1848

Poe writes of the death of his wife, Virginia.

"It is the nature of thought in general,
as it is in the nature of some ores in particular,
to be richest when most superficial."

**FROM A REVIEW OF MISS BARRETT'S
"THE DRAMA OF EXILE,"** *THE BROADWAY JOURNAL,*
JANUARY 4, 1845

CHAPTER
FOUR

MASTER
OF THE
MACABRE

"**I**t is impossible to say how first the idea entered my brain; but once conceived, it haunted me day and night."

"THE TELL-TALE HEART," 1843

"**A** large mirror—so at first it seemed to me in my confusion—now stood where none had been perceptible before; and, as I stepped up to it in extremity of terror, mine own image, but with features all pale and dabbled in blood, advanced to meet me with a feeble and tottering gait."

"WILLIAM WILSON," 1839

"**D**uring the whole of a dull, dark, and soundless day in the autumn of the year, when the clouds hung oppressively low in the heavens, I had been passing alone, on horseback, through a singularly dreary tract of country, and at length found myself, as the shades of the evening drew on, within view of the melancholy House of Usher."

"THE FALL OF THE HOUSE OF USHER,"
1839

Poe wrote some of his best-known tales between 1838 and 1844. They include:

The Fall of the House of Usher (1839)

The Murders in the Rue Morgue (1841)

The Masque of the Red Death (1842)

The Pit and the Pendulum (1842)

The Tell-Tale Heart (1843)

The Black Cat (1843)

The Gold Bug (1843)

"**D**ark draperies hung upon the walls. The general furniture was profuse, comfortless, antique, and tattered. Many books and musical instruments lay scattered about, but failed to give any vitality to the scene. I felt that I breathed an atmosphere of sorrow. An air of stern, deep, and irredeemable gloom hung over and pervaded all."

**"THE FALL OF THE HOUSE OF USHER,"
1839**

"**D**eep into that darkness peering, long
I stood there wondering, fearing,
Doubting, dreaming dreams no mortal ever
dared to dream before."

"THE RAVEN," 1845

The much-loved poet Henry Wadsworth Longfellow was often on the receiving end of Poe's brutal literary criticism. Poe once accused him of being the "GREAT MOGUL of the Imitators," or in other words, a plagiarist. After Poe's death, Longfellow wrote, "My works seemed to give him much trouble, first and last, but Mr. Poe is dead and gone, and I am alive and still writing, and that is the end of the matter."

"**F**or his gold I had no desire. I think it was his eye! yes, it was this! He had the eye of a vulture—a pale blue eye, with a film over it. Whenever it fell upon me, my blood ran cold; and so by degrees—very gradually—I made up my mind to take the life of the old man, and thus rid myself of the eye forever."

"THE TELL-TALE HEART," 1843

Illustration for "The Imp of the Perverse," by Arthur Rackham, 1935

"There is no passion in nature so demonically impatient, as that of him who, shuddering upon the edge of a precipice, thus meditates a plunge."

"THE IMP OF THE PERVERSE," 1845

"**H**ear the tolling of the bells -
Iron bells!
What a world of solemn thought their
monody compels!
In the silence of the night,
How we shiver with affright,
At the melancholy menace of their tone!"

"THE BELLS," 1849

"The eyes were lifeless, and lustreless, and seemingly pupilless, and I shrank involuntarily from their glassy stare to the contemplation of the thin and shrunken lips. They parted; and in a smile of peculiar meaning, the teeth of the changed Berenice disclosed themselves slowly to my view. Would to God that I had never beheld them, or that, having done so, I had died!"

"BERENICE," 1835

"But see, amid the mimic rout,
A crawling shape intrude!
A blood-red thing that writhes from out
The scenic solitude!
It writhes!—it writhes!—with mortal pangs
The mimes become its food,
And seraphs sob at vermin fangs
In human gore imbued…"

"THE CONQUEROR WORM," 1843

"It was hard by the dim lake of Auber,
In the misty mid region of Weir—
It was down by the dank tarn of Auber,
In the ghoul-haunted woodland of Weir."

"ULALUME," 1847

"And then there stole into my fancy, like a rich musical note, the thought of what sweet rest there must be in the grave."

"THE PIT AND THE PENDULUM," 1842

"**Y**ou have conquered, and I yield. Yet, henceforward art thou also dead—dead to the World, to Heaven and to Hope! In me didst thou exist—and, in my death, see by this image, which is thine own, how utterly thou hast murdered thyself."

"WILLIAM WILSON," 1839

"Upon the bed, before that whole company, there lay a nearly liquid mass of loathsome— of detestable putrescence."

**"THE FACTS IN THE CASE OF M. VALDEMAR,"
1845**

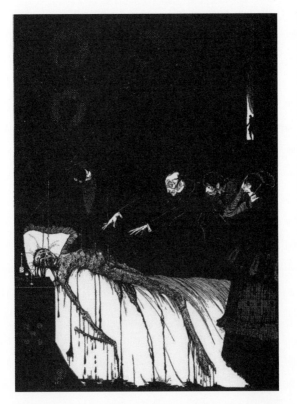

Illustration for "The Facts in the Case of M. Valdemar," by Harry Clarke, 1919

"The fury of a demon instantly possessed me. I knew myself no longer. My original soul seemed, at once, to take its flight from my body; and a more than fiendish malevolence, gin-nurtured, thrilled every fibre of my frame."

"THE BLACK CAT," 1843

"**A**nd the cloud that took the form
(When the rest of Heaven was blue)
Of a demon in my view."

"ALONE," MARCH 17, 1829

Written when Poe was 21, but not published until
September 1875, after his death.

"**S**o lovely was the loneliness
Of a wild lake, with black rock bound,
And the tall pines that tower'd around.
But when the Night had thrown her pall
Upon that spot, as upon all...
Then—ah then I would awake
To the terror of the lone lake."

"THE LAKE," 1828

"**W**hile, like a ghastly rapid river,
Through the pale door
A hideous throng rush out forever
And laugh—but smile no more."

"THE HAUNTED PALACE," 1839

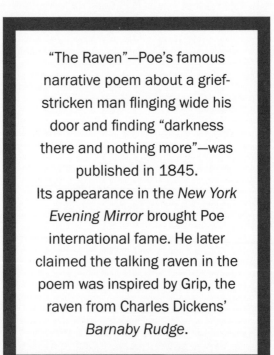

"The Raven"—Poe's famous narrative poem about a grief-stricken man flinging wide his door and finding "darkness there and nothing more"—was published in 1845.

Its appearance in the *New York Evening Mirror* brought Poe international fame. He later claimed the talking raven in the poem was inspired by Grip, the raven from Charles Dickens' *Barnaby Rudge*.

"Once upon a midnight dreary, while
I pondered, weak and weary,
Over many a quaint and curious volume
of forgotten lore—
While I nodded, nearly napping, suddenly
there came a tapping,
As of some one gently rapping, rapping
at my chamber door."

"THE RAVEN," 1845

" **I** have, indeed, no abhorrence of danger,
except in its absolute effect—in terror."

**"THE FALL OF THE HOUSE OF USHER,"
1839**

"The agony of my soul found vent in one loud, long and final scream of despair."

"THE PIT AND THE PENDULUM," 1842

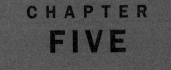

**POETRY AND
PROSE**

"Literature is the most noble of professions. In fact, it is about the only one fit for a man. For my own part, there is no seducing me from the path."

LETTER TO FREDERICK W. THOMAS, 1849

"I need scarcely observe that a poem deserves its title only inasmuch as it excites, by elevating the soul. The value of the poem is in the ratio of this elevating excitement. But all excitements are, through a psychal necessity, transient."

"THE POETIC PRINCIPLE," 1850

EDGAR ALLAN POE

"The death of a beautiful woman is, unquestionably, the most poetical topic in the world."

"THE PHILOSOPHY OF COMPOSITION,"
1846

"**W**ords have no power to impress the mind without the exquisite horror of their reality."

THE NARRATIVE OF ARTHUR GORDON PYM OF NANTUCKET, 1838

Poe is credited with inventing the modern detective story. "The Murders in the Rue Morgue" introduced readers to amateur sleuth C. Auguste Dupin along with the classic elements of future detective fiction. It was followed by two further detective tales, *The Mystery of Marie Rogêt* and *The Purloined Letter*. Arthur Conan Doyle, acknowledged Poe's influence on his famous fictional detective, Sherlock Holmes.

"**C**oincidences, in general, are great stumbling-blocks in the way of that class of thinkers who have been educated to know nothing of the theory of probabilities."

"THE MURDERS IN THE RUE MORGUE," 1841

"How many good books suffer neglect
through the inefficiency of their beginnings!"

"MARGINALIA," 1846

"**I** would define, in brief, the poetry of words as the rhythmical creation of beauty."

"THE POETIC PRINCIPLE," 1850

Illustration for "The Premature Burial," by Arthur Rackham, 1935

"**T**here are certain themes of which the interest is all-absorbing, but which are too entirely horrible for the purposes of legitimate fiction."

"THE PREMATURE BURIAL," 1844

"**N**othing is more clear than that every plot, worth the name, must be elaborated to its dénouement before anything be attempted with the pen. It is only with the dénouement constantly in view that we can give a plot its indispensable air of consequence, or causation, by making the incidents, and especially the tone at all points, tend to the development of the intention."

**"THE PHILOSOPHY OF COMPOSITION,"
1846**

"In criticism I will be bold, and as sternly, absolutely just with friend and foe. From this purpose nothing shall turn me."

**LETTER TO JOSEPH EVANS SNODGRASS,
JANUARY 18, 1841**

"In one case out of a hundred a point is excessively discussed because it is obscure; in the ninety-nine remaining it is obscure because excessively discussed."

"THE RATIONALE OF VERSE," 1846

"It is clear that a poem may be improperly brief. Undue brevity degenerates into mere epigrammatism. A very short poem, while now and then producing a brilliant or vivid, never produces a profound or enduring, effect. There must be the steady pressing down of the stamp upon the wax."

"THE POETIC PRINCIPLE," 1850

Poe coined the word
"tintinnabulation," which
describes the lingering sound of
a ringing bell that occurs once
it has been struck.

It appears in the first stanza
of his onomatopoeic poem
"The Bells".

"All the heavens, seem to twinkle
With a crystalline delight;
Keeping time, time, time,
In a sort of Runic rhyme,
To the tintinabulation that so musically wells
From the bells, bells, bells, bells,
Bells, bells, bells—
From the jingling and the tinkling of the bells."

"THE BELLS," 1849

"**M**usic, when combined with a pleasurable idea, is poetry; music without the idea is simply music; the idea without the music is prose from its very definitiveness."

"LETTER TO B –," 1836

"With me poetry has been not a purpose, but a passion; and the passions should be held in reverence: they must not—they cannot at will be excited, with an eye to the paltry compensations, or the more paltry commendations, of mankind."

PREFACE, *THE RAVEN AND OTHER POEMS*, 1845

" **A**s a poet and as a mathematician, he would reason well; as a mere mathematician, he could not have reasoned at all."

"THE PURLOINED LETTER," 1844

"**M**elancholy is ... the most legitimate of all the poetical tones."

"THE PHILOSOPHY OF COMPOSITION," 1846

"**B**eauty is the sole legitimate province of the poem."

**"THE PHILOSOPHY OF COMPOSITION,"
1846**

"These tales of ratiocination ['Murders in the Rue Morgue' and 'The Purloined Letter'] owe most of their popularity to being something in a new key ... People think they are more ingenious than they are—on account of their method and air of method ... Where is the ingenuity of unravelling a web which you yourself (the author) have woven for the express purpose of unravelling?"

LETTER TO PHILIP PENDLETON COOKE, AUGUST 9, 1846

CHAPTER
SIX

WIT AND
WISDOM

"**B**elieve nothing you hear, and only one half that you see."

"THE SYSTEM OF DOCTOR TARR AND PROFESSOR FETHER," 1845

"The true genius shudders at incompleteness, imperfection, and usually prefers silence to saying the something which is not everything that should be said."

MARGINALIA, 1844–49

"**A** wrong is unredressed when retribution overtakes its redresser. It is equally unredressed when the avenger fails to make himself felt as such to him who has done the wrong."

"THE CASK OF AMONTILLADO," 1846

Illustration for "The Cask of Amontillado," by Harry Clarke, 1919

"The Romans worshipped their standards; and the Roman standard happened to be an eagle. Our standard is only one-tenth of an Eagle—a Dollar—but we make all even by adoring it with ten-fold devotion."

MARGINALIA, 1844–49

"**Y**et if hope has flown away
In a night, or in a day,
In a vision, or in none,
Is it therefore the less gone?"

"A DREAM WITHIN A DREAM," 1849

Perhaps the greatest riddle of Poe's life is his death. In October 1849, he was discovered slumped in a Baltimore street, dressed in ill-fitting clothes that weren't his own. Admitted to hospital, Poe drifted in and out of consciousness, holding "vacant converse with spectral and imaginary objects on the walls." Unable to explain what had happened to him, he died a few days later at the age of 40.

"I intend to put up with nothing that I can put down (excuse the pun)..."

**LETTER TO JOHN BEAUCHAMP JONES,
AUGUST 8, 1839**

"**A** man's grammar, like Caesar's wife, must not only be pure, but above suspicion of impurity."

MARGINALIA, 1844–49

"There are chords in the hearts of the most reckless which cannot be touched without emotion."

**"THE MASQUE OF THE RED DEATH,"
1842**

"The customs of the world are so many conventional follies."

"THE SPECTACLES," 1844

Several theories have been put forward to explain Poe's mysterious death. Alcohol may have played a role, though a doctor who saw him stated there was no odor of alcohol on his breath. It has been suggested his delirium was caused by syphilis or rabies, while another theory suggests he was the victim of "cooping"—a form of election fraud where a kidnapped victim was drugged and made to cast several votes.

EDGAR ALLAN POE

"It is an evil growing out of our republican institutions, that here a man of large purse has usually a very little soul which he keeps in it."

**"THE PHILOSOPHY OF FURNITURE,"
BURTON'S GENTLEMAN'S MAGAZINE,
MAY 1840**

"**E**vil is a consequence of Good, so, in fact, out of Joy is sorrow born. Either the memory of past bliss is the anguish of to-day, or the agonies which are, have their origin in the ecstasies which might have been."

"BERENICE," 1835

"To vilify a great man is the readiest way in which a little man can himself attain greatness. The Crab might never have become a Constellation but for the courage it evinced in nibbling Hercules on the heel."

MARGINALIA, 1845

"**E**xperience has shown, and a true philosophy will always show, that a vast, perhaps the larger portion of the truth arises from the seemingly irrelevant."

"THE MYSTERY OF MARIE ROGÊT," 1842

"**D**ecorum—that bug-bear which deters so many from bliss until the opportunity for bliss has forever gone by."

"THE SPECTACLES," 1844

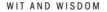

"The eye, like a shattered mirror, multiplies the images of sorrow."

"THE ASSIGNATION," 1834

Poe's great literary rival Rufus Wilmot Griswold wrote a damning obituary for his enemy.

It portrayed Poe as a mad alcoholic and opium addict who based his dark, disturbing tales on personal experience.

This distorted picture of the author has unfairly influenced popular opinion for more than a century.

"**H**e was at all times a dreamer—dwelling in ideal realms—in heaven or hell—peopled with creatures and the accidents of his brain. He walked the streets, in madness or melancholy, with lips moving in indistinct curses, or with eyes upturned in passionate prayers, (never for himself, for he felt, or professed to feel, that he was already damned)..."

RUFUS GRISWOLD

From his obituary for Poe, published in the *New York Daily Tribune*, October 9, 1849.

EDGAR ALLAN POE

"**T**hat man is not truly brave who is afraid either to seem or to be, when it suits him, a coward."

MARGINALIA, 1846

"**T**o observe attentively is to remember distinctly."

**"THE MURDERS IN THE RUE MORGUE,"
1841**

Illustration for "Hop-Frog," by Arthur Rackham, 1935

"**W**hether people grow fat by joking, or whether there is something in fat itself which predisposes to a joke, I have never been quite able to determine; but certain it is that a lean joker is a *rara avis in terris*."

"HOP-FROG," 1849

"**M**r. Briggs has never composed in his life three consecutive sentences of grammatical English ... His conversation has now and then the merit of humor, but he has a perfect mania for contradiction, and it is impossible to utter an uninterrupted sentence in his hearing."

**FROM "CHARLES F. BRIGGS"
IN "THE LITERATI OF NEW YORK CITY," 1846**

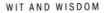
"**M**an is an animal that diddles, and there is no animal that diddles but man.

**"DIDDLING CONSIDERED AS ONE OF THE
EXACT SCIENCES," 1843**

Despite his prolific literary output, Poe was initially buried in an unmarked grave in Baltimore Presbyterian Cemetery.

In 1875, a new monument was erected. Poet Walt Whitman attended the ceremony, and Alfred Tennyson wrote an epitaph.

"**F**ate that once denied him,
And envy that once decried him,
And malice that belied him,
Now cenotaph his fame."

ALFRED TENNYSON'S EPITAPH FOR POE

"**M**r. Clark once did me the honor to review my poems, and—I forgive him."

FROM "LEWIS GAYLORD CLARK" IN "THE LITERATI OF NEW YORK CITY," 1846

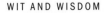

"To die laughing must be the most glorious of all glorious deaths!"

"THE ASSIGNATION," 1834

"When I say, "no precise character," I mean that Mr. C., as a literary man, has about him no determinateness, no distinctiveness, no saliency of point;—an apple, in fact, or a pumpkin, has more angles. He is as smooth as oil or a sermon from Doctor Hawks; he is noticeable for nothing in the world except for the markedness by which he is noticeable for nothing."

**FROM "LEWIS GAYLORD CLARK" IN
"THE LITERATI OF NEW YORK CITY", 1846**

"**E**ach person, in his own estimate, is the pivot on which all the rest of the world spins round."

**FROM A REVIEW OF
J. R. LOWELL'S "A FABLE FOR CRITICS,"
MARCH 1849**

"Is all that we see or seem
But a dream within a dream?"

"A DREAM WITHIN A DREAM," 1849